THE LAST BODY PART

Sarajane Woolf is an essayist whose work has appeared in *The Christian Science Monitor*, *Alaska Quarterly Review*, *Ecotone*, *South Dakota Review*, *The Broome Review*, and *North Dakota Quarterly*. Her *South Dakota Review* piece was named a "Notable Essay" by Robert Atwan, Series Editor, *Best American Essays*. She lives with her husband, Nick, in Carpinteria, California and is currently writing a book on the London churches designed by Sir Christopher Wren, *The Wren Church Variations*.

D1041906

First published by GemmaMedia in 2012.

GemmaMedia
230 Commercial Street
Boston, MA 02109 USA

www.gemmamedia.com

Printed in the United States of America

16   15   14   13   12   1   2   3   4   5

978-1-936846-30-6

Library of Congress Cataloging-in-Publication Data

Woolf, Sarajane.
    The last body part / Sarajane Woolf.
        p. cm. — (Gemma open door)
    ISBN 978-1-936846-30-6
    1. Parathyroid glands. 2. Parathyroid glands—Surgery.
    I. Title.
    QP188.P3W66 2012
    612.4'48—dc23

                                        2012031887

Cover by Night & Day Design

Inspired by the Irish series of books designed for adult literacy, Gemma Open Door Foundation provides fresh stories, new ideas, and essential resources for young people and adults as they embrace the power of reading and the written word.

Brian Bouldrey
North American Series Editor

GEMMA

Open Door

for Nick

One Man's Trash

On November 19, 1849, a male rhino tripped and fell at the London Zoo. He hit the ground hard and cracked a rib, which stabbed one of his lungs. The next day, the zookeeper saw him try to vomit. Blood and mucus shot out of his nose and mouth. A week later, the rhino died.

How would you get rid of a dead two-ton rhino? The zookeeper got rid of him the same way we'd get rid of an old couch or fridge. He offered the rhino for free. "You haul him, he's yours," the zookeeper said.

You know that saying, "One man's trash is another man's treasure"? In this case, one man's dead rhino was another man's . . . I'm tempted to say *rhinestone*. But this was true treasure to the right man, a free two-ton diamond. That man was the scientist and professor Richard Owen, head of the Hunterian Museum in London.

Richard Owen had urged the London Zoo to buy the rhino ten years earlier, even though rhinos don't come cheap, so he was sad that the animal died at a younger age than expected. But he jumped at the chance to dissect any dead animal. He would measure all the organs. He'd study how the pieces of the animal fit together, as if it were a puzzle. Then he'd write a scientific paper on what he'd learned.

If you've ever dissected a worm, you

know it can be hard to find their tiny body parts, like the brain. Imagine Richard Owen dissecting the rhino. Organs that get lost in a worm are huge in a two-ton animal. He even found a gland that no one had ever noticed before—not in any animal, not in any human. The gland was the size of a plump green pea. I saw this gland at the Hunterian Museum in London, preserved in a jar.

Where My Story Begins

My road to the rhino gland started at a free health fair. At 6:30 one Saturday morning, I left home without eating only to stand in a long, long line. Who were all those people, awake and dressed at that hour? I inched to the front of the line. There, a young man in a crisp white coat tried to take my blood. Not until his third sharp jab into my arm did his syringe fill with a deep red.

A month later the results of the blood test came in the mail. I tore into the envelope as if it held a report card that would reveal my bright future or punish me for my past. How did my body do this year? Numbers that were too big or too small were lined up on the far right. Some I don't worry about. I'm not going to stop eating butter and ice cream just because a number is high. But I saw something new on that list: high calcium. That's good, right? I eat yogurt every day and swallow calcium pills because calcium builds bones. Didn't seem like a bad thing to have high calcium.

"Don't worry. It's not cancer," my

doctor said when I showed him the results of the test. *Of course not*, I thought. *It's just calcium.* How little I knew. He pulled a book off a shelf and opened it to a line drawing of the inside of a neck. Then he pointed to a small oval shape filled in with the color red. And, for the first time, I heard the name of the gland that Richard Owen found in his rhino: *parathyroid.*

A bad name, if there ever was one. The Greek word *para* means *beside* or *near*. So *parathyroid* means *near the thyroid*. True, these glands are near the thyroid. But this is like naming your son for the boy next door, calling him Para-Bob or Para-Sam. The name made sense to someone. Maybe because blood vessels connect the thyroid and parathyroid, like water and sewer pipes that serve both your house and the one next door. Still, every other organ in the body gets its own name. And never mind that a number of lofty words start with *para*, like *paramedic*. To me, *para* sounds like trouble. Think *parasite* or *paranoia*. See what I mean? So for now, I'll give the parathyroid gland a nickname—the PT gland.

Built-In Spare Parts

Most of us have four PT glands. They're tucked behind the thyroid, arranged in pairs on each side of the windpipe in an upper and a lower set. Often the size of a small grain of rice, they can look pear-shaped or flat like a lentil. Their color varies from a grayish white to a reddish brown. Fat can make them look yellow.

In any case, their color is not the same as the thyroid's, which makes the smooth, shiny glands easier for a surgeon to see.

The glands control calcium in the blood. If the level is too low, they secrete a hormone that tells the bones to release calcium. If the level is too high, the glands sit back and wait for it to drop. Just like a heater with a thermostat.

The four glands all do the same thing. So one can go bad—and by that I mean it can have a benign tumor—and it's no big deal to take it out. We're born with built-in spare parts. A great design, except for one glitch. The four glands work like old Christmas lights. One burnt bulb makes the whole string go dark. In our bodies, one bad PT gland makes the other three shut down. Worse than that, the gland with the tumor goes into overdrive. It no longer responds to small changes in the level of blood calcium. Instead, the gland shovels the PT hormone into the blood whether it needs calcium or not. Blood calcium stays high, as my health-fair test showed. And the bones weaken as they keep sloughing off calcium. Surgery to remove the bad gland is the only way to stop the body from turning into a creature without a skeleton.

A Bat in a Cave

My doctor sent me to a cancer center for a scan of my neck to find which of my four PT glands had gone bad. First, someone inserted an IV feed into my arm and injected me with radioactive slime. Next, I was led to a room filled with scratched machines painted the colors of old gym lockers. A technician hauled in a heavy lens on a beat-up cart. The lens looked like a light for a stage or a TV studio, but bigger. When she tried to change the lens on my machine, it jammed. The process was awkward, like kicking the legs shut on a heavy folding table. The place could have been a set for *Star Wars*—everything both old and space-age new. An alien could have come in for a scan of an organ vital for X-ray vision or for beaming a message to Mars.

When a second technician tried to strap down my arms, I protested. She believed me when I said I'd lie still. I kept my word, but it was hard because a large camera hovered over my face and neck for a long time. During the scan, the technician asked once if I was OK. When I said "Yes," my voice bounced back too fast from the camera, as if I were a bat in a cave, too close to a wall. At one point I swallowed, and my throat rose just enough to touch something metal.

I moved to a second camera that would photograph my neck from a different angle for a full twenty minutes. Flat plates moved in an arc around my head. On the sides, they bumped my shoulders, as if the space were too crowded for both of us.

A third technician pulled out my IV and told me to put pressure on a cotton pad over the wound. Then she led me to another room, left, and didn't return. Feeling abandoned after all the earlier attention, I stepped into the hallway. A fourth technician, one I hadn't seen before, gave me a puzzled look. I said, "I guess I'm done," and walked away.

To Boldly Go

Most body parts are stuck in their assigned spots; the brain in the head, the heart in the chest, the stomach in the stomach. Before birth, the PT glands are not stuck—they're more like free agents. They start growing near the tube that connects the nose and mouth. About the fifth week in the life of a fetus, the glands get restless. Then they break away and head south.

Another gland, the thymus, heads down at the same time. The PT glands should stop at the thyroid. But sometimes the two lower glands keep moving with the thymus. They boldly go where PT glands aren't meant to go. This doesn't create problems. It's just a bit odd. In one study of fifty-four cases of PT glands on the loose, twelve sets were found between the lungs. For this tiny gland, that's a long way to go. If your stomach moved an equivalent distance, you'd find it past your feet.

A sea captain with the U.S. Merchant Marine, Charles Martell, had the first known case of a bad runaway PT gland. Between 1918 and 1926, he had eight bone fractures and shrank seven inches, signs of a PT problem. Surgeons opened up his neck six times. But they couldn't find the bad gland—like the gas station attendant who opened the front hood of my VW and couldn't find the engine.

Charles read anatomy books in his free time. He decided he had a tumor in his chest. In the seventh operation, surgeons found the bad PT gland right where Charles said it was. The machines that found my tumor wouldn't have known where to find his.

TWO

Two Forms of ID

When I worry, I turn to words. Not the spoken kind, but the kind piled on pages in a set order. So when I knew I needed PT surgery, I made my way to a library. But not just any library. This was the British Library in London—more like a church for those who worship books. These books are all the more dear for the fact that not just anyone can walk in and touch them.

Getting a British Library card is not as much work as getting a driver's license, and not as fussy as getting a passport. But it's hard in a weird way, because you can't just *want* the card. Wanting a driver's license or a passport is good enough. But wanting to read the books in the British Library? You better have a good excuse. Waiting in line to get a library card is not as long a process as waiting in line at your local DMV, but the look of dread on each face is the same. At the DMV: What if I don't pass the driver's test? At the British Library: What if they don't like my reason for wanting a card?

The best plan is to say you need the card for research. A letter from someone official that says you need this card can help too. Plus, wear a clean shirt. Brush your hair. Smile. Don't look scary. And bring two forms of ID. Not DVD rental cards from stores that have closed, but a driver's license and a passport. Next thing you know, you're smiling into a tiny camera mounted on the desk. Then out pops a card, your photo looking like they used a fish-eye lens, your nose much larger than you imagined.

The reward is that you can wander the book stacks. Or you can fill out a form asking to have books sent back from overflow storage. Some books are stored in the town of Boston Spa. These books sip perfect gin and tonics while getting foot massages. They arrive at the library well rested, eager for you to read them.

I found the shelves where medical books are kept. No need to send away to the spa. For days I read the easy parts of two books about surgery of the PT glands. One was written in 2007, the other in 1910. I copied sentences about Richard Owen and his dissected rhino. I learned that he found the first PT gland in 1850. He didn't call it that. He didn't call it anything except *small*, *compact*, and *yellow*. I don't blame him. As my mother-in-law would say, "He had other fish to fry." Or beasts to dissect.

No one else gave any thought to the gland for almost four decades. Then, in 1887 a Swedish student, Ivar Sandström, wrote about seeing the same kind of gland in fifty human bodies. His paper had the enticing title: "On a New Gland in Man." But no one seemed to care.

What Are These?
(A Brief History of PT Research)

How do you figure out the purpose of a new gland? Early scientists were like kids sticking bobby pins into power outlets to see what might happen. In this case they pulled those tiny glands out to see what came next. What came next was not pretty. A Frenchman named Eugene Gley took the glands out of some rabbits in 1891. The effect was the same on all of them: tetany, meaning strong muscle pain and spasms. If you've had cramps in your legs, you've had a taste of tetany. You can die from tetany and hundreds of lab animals did. The death toll from the books I read included over 300 dogs, 159 rabbits, 81 rats, 68 mice,

38 cats, 5 foxes, 1 goat, 1 monkey, 1 prairie wolf, 1 turtle, and an unknown number of birds.

A year later an Austrian, Anton von Eiselsberg, took one step beyond Gley's work. First he cut out the PT glands from a cat, but when the cat got tetany, he put the glands back in the animal. He wanted to see if the cramps stopped. They did, though this seems like the obvious outcome.

By the early 1900s, scientists put all their efforts into getting rid of tetany. Some implanted PT glands, just as von Eiselsberg did. Others fed PT glands to lab animals who had tetany. S.P. Beebe invented a recipe for extract of beef PT glands that he injected into dogs:

Clean the glands and cut into small
    pieces.

Grind with a mortar and some
    sand until the mass is moist and
    pasty.

Add a salt solution that is six to
    eight times the volume of the
    gland-paste.

Add two drops of ten percent
    sodium hydroxide.

Refrigerate for eighteen to thirty-
    six hours.

Strain using gauze to remove the
    fat and any coarse tissue.

Strain a second time using thick
    paper.

Preserve the final extract by adding
    chloroform. Store at low
    temperature.

I know I saw a similar recipe by some-one—Julia Child?—using an organ meat, maybe tongue or liver.

An American named Carl Voegtlin took his study in a new and vital direction. In 1908, he learned that tetany could be stopped by feeding his victims calcium. Got milk? Got cheese? Got ice cream? Still, no one knew where the PT glands fit in. What did they have to do with calcium? The scientist Jacob Erdheim saw that people with larger-than-normal PT glands—glands with tumors—had problems with their bones. Some had soft bones. Others had bones that were deformed. He thought bone disease made the PT glands swell. He didn't offer any proof of this. But everyone just said, "Oh, OK," and kept saying that for almost twenty years.

In 1925, Dr. Felix Mandl tried to cure a patient who had bone pain, a broken femur, and high blood calcium. The doctor thought these problems made the PT gland not work right. He put new PT tissue into the man, but that didn't help. A lightbulb flashed in his mind. He saw that everyone had the story backward. A PT gland with a tumor caused the bone problem, not the other way around. He cut into the patient's neck and took out the bad gland. This was the first successful operation to remove a PT gland. His patient died a few years later. That wasn't Mandl's fault. The patient might have had the first known case of PT cancer, not just a benign tumor, so taking out the PT gland didn't solve the problem. To me, Mandl was still a hero.

THREE

Surgeons Who Swim

I once asked an astrologer if he saw any danger in my future. He told me to be wary of people who wouldn't look me in the eye. That could be half the world, so I ignored that advice. He also said to watch out for surgeons who swim. I hadn't thought of that for a long time. Then as I waited to meet, for the first time, the surgeon who would operate on me, I felt a sudden dread. I wished I'd never been warned about swimming surgeons. And unless he had swimming medals hanging on his office wall, how would I know?

I expected the surgeon to tell me

about the function of the PT gland. I hoped he'd also tell me about Richard Owen's rhino. I thought of the fun I'd have saying that I'd seen the actual rhino PT gland. I pictured the kind of talk you have with new friends when you learn that you like the same books or music or movies. Maybe he'd read the 1910 surgery book that I read. He'd tell me about early research on animals, about scientists ripping out all the PT glands. "Not a good idea!" I'd say. I wanted him to see that I knew a bit about this gland, that I wasn't going into surgery blind.

"He didn't say one thing about the rhino," I told my husband later. "Not one. So I couldn't bring it up. But he looked me in the eye," I was happy to report. "And there were no swimming medals on the wall or around his neck, Mark Spitz style. No whiff of chlorine from a morning swim."

"Were his eyes bloodshot?" my husband asked.

"I couldn't tell behind his glasses," I said.

I liked the surgeon. But I was sorry later that I hadn't looked at his hands, to see if I thought they were up to the task of cutting out my gland. I'd hate to see that they looked like a carpenter's or a gardener's hands. I'd want to see a pianist's long, slender fingers. Hands that could perform tiny tasks, like fixing watches. And I failed to ask how many PT surgeries he'd done. I'd feared that might break some code of trust.

On-the-Job Training

My surgeon may not have belonged to the world's oldest profession, but it's still an old trade. Men who were one step past apes knew how to lop off a bad leg with an axe made of stone. Later, they learned how to cut into bodies to pull out bad organs. Bits of history from India and Egypt show that long before the Christian era, surgeons cut out tumors and fixed hernias. They even did nose jobs for men who'd had them bashed in as a penalty for adultery. The Greeks and Romans had keen surgical-knife skills too. Plus they knew more than anyone up to that point about germs and how to prevent infections.

Then came the Dark Ages, in the fourth century AD. Earth had a culture crash, much like a power outage, and all that surgery know-how was lost. Over the next thousand years, surgery skills grew again. In England and France a trade known as the barber-surgeon arose. You could get a haircut, a shave, and a vital organ removed by the same person. Makes sense when you think about it—barbers owned the sharp knives and scissors.

For longer than you might imagine, barbers had higher status than surgeons. Both learned their trades through on-the-job training. Doctors had an even higher status. They needed an advanced degree, so they ruled from the top of the medical totem pole. Even now in England, only doctors use the title Dr., while surgeons use Mr., Miss, Mrs., or Ms.

Time Travel

Reading a quick history of surgery, it's easy to feel superior to the greatest minds of yesterday. Why did it take scientists so long to learn how blood moved through the body? Why did it take even longer to learn about germs? Then I saw that the British Library books I read on PT surgery, written in 1910 and 2007, had one thing in common. Both exuded the joy of knowing more about the PT gland than anyone on Earth had ever known.

A reader is a time traveler peeking into the past. But the 1910 book looked brand new. The cover had been replaced, and the spine had not yet been cracked. So when I opened the book, I had no sense of stepping back in time. I jumped fresh and innocent into each chapter.

Like everyone who read the book in 1910, I read cutting-edge research. The *Back to the Future* fellows took their digital watches and Calvin Klein underwear into the past. I went nowhere, took nothing. My smug attitude vanished.

Back in my twenty-first century surgeon's office, the ultrasound image of my neck looked primitive—like a static voice across the first phone line. "See that kidney-bean shape?" he asked, pointing on the screen. His finger blocked my view, so I wasn't sure if I did. He moved so I could see better. Then he showed me on the screen how my pencil-thick jugular vein crushed when he lightly pushed on my neck. Once I'd seen that, he pointed to my PT gland again. Enlarged by the tumor and magnified on the screen, it was anything but tiny. More the size of a prize-winning bean. Or a rhino's PT gland.

Crawling with Germs

It only strikes me now as odd that I have no idea where my surgery was performed. I know the hospital, of course, but not which room. Where was I wheeled after the drug injected through my IV made me lose all awareness? How many people were in the room? Was surgery a small affair with just me, the surgeon, and one or two others? I'll never know. But I'm sure that the scene was nothing like surgery in London's Old Operating Theatre.

Tucked into the attic of an old church next to a hospital, the space is now a museum. But from 1822 until about

1867, limbs were cut off, broken bones set, and surface wounds mended here. Patients weren't cut open, because infections from germs meant certain death. Students could watch from the floor or from raised u-shaped rows of seating. They packed in the room like herrings, said one surgeon from that era. On some days people had to be kicked out to allow the surgeon room to move around the table. Students talked during surgery, sometimes yelling for others to move so they could see.

The room was anything but sterile. Skylights lit the wooden operating table in the center of the room. During surgery, a blanket was put over the table and an oilcloth on top. Below the table was a wooden box filled with sawdust.

The surgeon kicked it around to catch dripping blood. A helper stirred the blood and sawdust until it turned into a mush, then tossed it out and added fresh dust. One writer of the time said a surgeon's coat was stiff with pus and blood. Patients were as likely to get infected from the surgeon, who may or may not have washed his hands, as from his tools or one of the students. You can almost feel germs crawling around the room.

Elizabeth Raigen, age sixty, was a typical patient. In 1824 the wheel of a passing horse-drawn cart injured her leg. She had an open wound and a fracture just above her ankle. A surgeon pulled the gaping wound together as best he could. The wound oozed a foul pus, and the patient's tongue dried out and turned brown. The only chance to save her life was to chop off her leg above the knee. She sipped wine and brandy to numb the pain. Soon after the operation, she died, likely from infections. The practice of surgery was shut down here once the idea of germs was understood.

Say the Name Out Loud

A friend of mine had PT surgery almost twenty years ago. Before the big day, her surgeon said to her, "There's a chance I might cut your vocal chords, and you'll never speak again." Like cutting the strings of a violin. It might be more correct to say he could cut the laryngeal nerve, but that's what she remembers.

These days no one dies of PT surgery. But no one wants the nerve to the vocal chords cut. One problem is that the nerve is more like the lacy branches of a tree than it is like a tree trunk. The modern surgery book I read said that a surgeon should have a "profound knowledge" of anatomy. The book went on to say that the surgeon should point out the nerve before cutting out the bad gland, calling this practice the "gold standard." I pictured a surgeon calling out the names of body parts during surgery but feeling a bit silly about the whole thing.

Cutting the nerve to the vocal chords isn't the only problem, I read. The surgeon may clamp or stretch the nerve and not know that it's being damaged. But after surgery the patient can't talk. In a few weeks, the nerve could bounce back. The book says to wait six to twelve months before panicking. If you still can't talk, you never will.

When I asked my surgeon about the laryngeal nerve, he said that these days the nerve wasn't a problem in PT surgery, although it can be with thyroid surgery. He also said that a bad PT gland tends to pop right out. This made me think of tiddlywinks. I still walked away hoping that when he cut into my neck he'd look for the laryngeal nerve, then say the name out loud.

FOUR

Dead Tadpoles

When Richard Owen is given the dead rhino, he lives and works at the Royal College of Surgeons. He and his wife, Caroline, have a cramped apartment on the second floor. Caroline lives with dead animals her entire married life. In 1836, a year after her wedding, she writes in her diary, "Last night a kangaroo (dead) came to R. from the zoo." That morning Richard dissects some threadlike worms from the kangaroo. Caroline says he opened them in a clever way to show their beautiful, almost clear insides. I picture these worms on their dining room table.

In the next few years, an ostrich, a wombat, a giraffe, a hippo, a 15-foot boa, a lion—"poor George"—and a sloth die. Some of these beasts are dissected at the zoo. But most of them come home with Richard. Their son, Willy, likes to watch his dad work. After dissecting a chimp, Richard says that seven-year-old Willy smells like he soaked in the same rum preservative as the chimp.

Richard and Caroline host live animals also. On June 18, 1842, Caroline writes, "Dr. Martin Barry came in from Jersey. He brought two green lizards for me, and some tadpoles (all dead but two)." Green lizards are a great gift idea. But why would a man give a woman dead tadpoles?

One day, someone leaves two

hampers at the door. One holds dead fish, the other a live bird. Richard and Caroline learn that a fisherman found them. The fish tried to eat the bird, but it got stuck in the fish's throat. Another day, a Dr. and Mrs. Buckland stop by with two of their boys and two live marmots. Caroline writes, "The Doctor sat on the sofa with the two marmots and his bag on his lap." She finds this scene as funny as we might. After the guests leave with their marmots, saying they have tickets for the theatre, Caroline adds, "I don't know if the marmots are going too!"

Dancing the Polka

On May 23, 1846, Caroline visits the zoo. She writes that the rhino looked pleased with himself, standing in water, "like a clumsy model of a creature in mud." She also says that the elephant is ill. A week later the elephant dies. Richard sends some students to take out the elephant's brain, but they find it too hard. The next day, Richard saws through the skull himself. When he tries to pull the brains out, he gets bone splinters in his hands. Caroline says it was pouring wet that day. Richard must have been soaked. On June 11, the dead elephant arrives at their apartment. Caroline calmly notes, "The defunct elephant made me keep all the windows open." She also says she "got R. to smoke cigars all over the house" to help get rid of the smell. Think of that the next time someone in your household fails to take out the garbage.

Two years later the zoo's rhino dies from his fall. The same scene repeats. Caroline says she hears "a great trampling and rushing upstairs past our bedroom door." She asks Richard if men are "dancing the polka on the stairs." He says the men are carrying the body up. "They'll be dissecting for fellowship to-day!" he adds. These sound like code words for a grisly party. The next day Caroline writes about the large number of "defunct" rhino parts. History books don't always record facts like this: someone has to live with the smell of a rotting rhino before the PT gland can be discovered.

When the zoo first wanted to buy the rhino, Richard inspected him by poking his thick hide. He said the rhino was healthy and would live many years. At his new home, the rhino ate giant portions of hay, oats, rice, carrots, and bread. When the rhino dies, Richard writes to his sisters, calling the rhino an "old friend and client." He also says he's been too busy after the death to deal with "mundane relations, sisters included." Richard's only comfort, he says, is that his study of the rhino's organs will "furnish forth an immortal" paper.

A Mystery

Maybe not immortal, but Richard Owen's 1850 paper is still available today. At the British Library I find "On

the Anatomy of the Indian Rhinoceros"
on microfilm. My copy is fuzzy, like TV
in the 1950s.

I flip through the drawings of rhino
parts in Richard's paper. Could these
have been Caroline's work? She often
drew parts of animals that Richard dissected. She draws a shark's head for him
one day. And on July 21, 1836, she works
all day "drawing a wombat's brain for R."
Then R. himself comes home and says
it was "all wrong." So Caroline has to
start over. How can he think she drew
the brain wrong? Isn't any brain a mess
of curvy lines like a pile of cooked spa-
ghetti? I start to see Richard as a bit fussy
and Caroline as much more fun.

I wish I could find proof that the
rhino drawings are Caroline's. Her diary

is no help. She offers evidence that Richard knows how to draw, so they might be his. On October 23, 1838, she writes in her diary, "In the morning R. drew a diagram of an octopus." Yet, on December 27, Caroline ". . . made two ink outlines of shark's teeth." Sometimes Richard and Caroline work together. On April 10, 1844, Richard draws the outline for something that Caroline colors before one of his lectures.

We'll never know what that drawing showed. But we do know that the rhino drawings are detailed works of art. The bladder is as lovely as a jellyfish. The colon is almost handsome. And who knew that a tonsil could be gorgeous, a stomach compelling? Or that the inside of the small intestine looks like a cozy shag rug?

An article in a 1911 newsletter from Johns Hopkins Hospital says that Caroline helped her husband "in no small degree by her powers of observation and by her artistic skill." Could this mean that Caroline might have spotted the small yellow PT gland before Richard did? He may have been distracted by the larger organs. And if she was eager to draw the gland for Richard's immortal paper, she may have given in to his veto. The thyroid is there. So are the vocal chords. But nothing that looks like a newly found gland.

What Richard Knows

I skim the text of Richard's paper, in search of the PT gland. As I read, I see the vast range of his knowledge. Richard knows that dead elephants rot faster than cud-chewing beasts, such as cows. He knows that a dead two-toed sloth stays "sweet" for a long time, even in hot weather. He knows that a rhino's anus can open to "a great extent," for "large masses" of feces. He says that you need a chisel to remove rhino hide from a skull.

The paper is not easy to read. Too many words like *aponeuroses* (where a muscle becomes a tendon). Or *tegumentary prepuce* (penis foreskin). I wish I could change the meaning of one word I learned—*epiploon*. Now it means "tissue that connects the stomach and liver." But I want it to mean something that I use daily. Then I could say, "My epiploon this, my epiploon that." Otherwise, for me it's a wasted word. "No trace of an epiploon," Richard writes.

The numbers in Richard's paper are huge. The rhino's spleen weighs five pounds. The kidney weighs eleven. The heart, twenty-eight. The aorta is so large that Richard can insert his finger. The rectum is sixteen inches around. When Richard writes about the organs, he tells a daring story set in a giant's world. When he says, "The spleen and kidneys were brought into view," I see him in a boat at the bend of a tropical river. When he reaches the first fold of the colon—over six feet long—I wonder how this will end for our hero. I shudder when he says that the colon was hard to move due to the weight of its contents.

The entire colon is twenty-five feet long. The biggest part could hold a man with room to spare. I'd rather be swallowed by a whale.

In Part III of Richard's paper, I find what I'm looking for. The PT gland is not given a name. The gland isn't even given a full sentence. Instead, a few words are attached to a sentence about the thyroid, and all he says is that he found a small yellow gland attached to the thyroid. He goes on to write in a dry, unsexy way about the sex organs of rhinos. Anyone reading the details—three feet nine inches long!—will soon forget about that small gland. And everyone does, for thirty-seven years.

Does the scant mention of the gland mean that Richard writes that half sentence only for Caroline's sake—maybe just after he vetoes her drawing the gland? If he cares about the gland, why doesn't he include as much detail about it as he does about the left lobe of the liver?

Richard and Caroline have no way of knowing the role of the PT gland. So the lack of fanfare about this find is no surprise. They also do not know that they've found the rhino version of the last major body part that will later be found in humans. Not that this should change anything. Consider the treatment of a first and last child. The first one's every breath is noted. The last one? Not so much. The gland needs a PR plan if it's ever going to have the attention it deserves. I'd start with giving it a new name, anything that doesn't include the word *thyroid*.

Name That Gland

I say something about the PT gland to a couple I've just met, using the full word *parathyroid*. The man says, "We have problems with ours."

"You do?" I ask. I read that having a bad PT gland is as likely as being struck by lighting. I question those odds. In the small town where I live, I know two people who've had PT surgery, but I don't know anyone who's been struck by lightning. And, I don't believe these people have both been struck with PT problems.

But his wife says, "Yes, a problem with my thyroid."

He nods and says, "Yes, me too, my thyroid."

"But I'm talking about the *para*thyroid," I say. They nod in a kind way, as if we all know I mean the thyroid, and I've added *para* on a whim.

The PT glands are sometimes called "the Glands of Owen." A bit awkward for a name. "Owen's Gland" works well, meaning just one gland or all four. Or even simpler—how about "Owen"? If I said I had an Owen removed, I bet not one person would mistake this for the thyroid. Plus, the rhyming options for poetry or songs are better with "Owen." Since kidney stones are a sign of a PT problem, how about this for a start:

I'm having dreadful problems with my Owen; I fear I might have grown a kidney stone.

Aching bones, another sign of a bad PT, could be worked in with the word *moan*. With *parathyroid*, your rhyming options may be limited to words like *android* or *hemorrhoid*. Those words are not likely to inspire a top-ten tune.

In the 1890s, the PT gland was called "Gley's Gland" for the Frenchman Eugene Gley. He's the one who ripped PT glands out of rabbits and proved that this causes tetany. Later, naming body parts for people fell out of fashion. Who knew? *Parathyroid* was the fall-back option.

I like the sound of "Gley's Gland," but I don't think Gley deserves more credit than Richard Owen. And rather than name it for Richard, I'd name the gland for Caroline. I'm holding out that she's the one who first sees the small yellow gland. She's the one who knows that the gland barely mentioned by Richard is the most important part of the two-ton rhino. Plus, she's the one with the sense of humor about living with a steady stream of dead body parts in her home. How about "Caroline's Gland" or just "Caroline"? I'd even be fine with "the Glands of Caroline."

FIVE

We Don't Have Time

In the way that a wedding, birth, or death can take over one's life, I let PT surgery overtake me. And just as a bride might find a poem to be read at her wedding, I found the perfect surgery poem: "On the Way to the Doctor's" by the poet and novelist Jim Harrison. Two lines in the prose poem inspired trust in my surgeon:

> Three of the surgeons don't have medical degrees but are part-time amateurs trying to learn the ropes. One is a butcher who wants to move up.

The final lines would protect me, like an actor told to "break a leg":

> . . . the seven surgeons are rolling up their sleeves, hot to get started. "We don't have time to wash our hands," they say in unison.

When the time came for me to be wheeled into surgery, I planned to repeat like a mantra: "We don't have time to wash our hands; we don't have time to wash our hands." Surely these words would keep me from leaving the hospital with a worse problem than the one I brought in.

We've Come to a Spa

On the day of my surgery, my husband and I walked in the front door of the hospital before dawn and found—no one. The lobby was dimly lit. No one greeted us. No distant sounds hinted that I was expected. Like we'd gotten the date wrong. Or come far too early for a party. If you're like me, you wonder if you can sneak away, hoping no one sees you so you don't have to admit your mistake. But you're still curious. You walk in, find yourself in the kitchen. The hosts are frosting a cake, pulling pizza out of the oven, uncorking a wine bottle. They're happy to see you; they think you came early to help. You're asked to spear chunks of raw meat and green peppers and onions with a sharp pointed stick. You don't feel out of place once you get to work. In the hospital we walked down a series of long halls, turning corners here and there. Finally we found a nurse, who took me to my room.

Dressed in a hospital gown, I waited lying down on a wheeled cart. My husband sat beside me in a rigid chair. Soon, a young woman with a kind manner brought flannel blankets into the room. The blankets were thin, but they'd been heated. Wrapped around me, they felt like a blessing. Three months ago I hadn't let my arms be strapped down for my neck scan. Now I welcomed this tight blanket cocoon. A second blanket over the first one sealed in the heat. "We've come to a spa!" I said to my husband. "All you need are the cucumbers," said the kind woman.

"How are the blankets heated?" I asked. She said, "They're kept in something like a refrigerator, only it's warm." Right there in my room, the word *refrigerator* morphed into a name for a heated box. In the room next to me, I'd overheard a woman say she would lose a third of her colon that day. When I heard her say the word *burrito*, I knew she'd had the same hot blanket treatment.

Another woman came in and jabbed me twice, trying to insert an IV feed. Not just a light prick, this hurt. She gave up. I liked her for that small favor. A moment later I heard "shit shit shit" from the woman next door, suggesting a problem with her IV feed too. Then it was time for me to be wheeled to the anesthesia room where someone else would push in the IV. My cart formed a slow-moving train with a number of other carts. Our loved ones walked by our sides. I pictured our train picking up speed, our loved ones running, waving goodbye. At a corner the young man pushing my cart said to my husband, "You can kiss her now." He obeyed. I'm glad he was told what to do. This was our first trip to the land of surgery, and we weren't sure how to behave.

That Blessed Chloroform

England's Queen Victoria wrote in her diary that she had been given "that blessed chloroform" during the birth of her eighth child in 1853. She called it "soothing" and "delightful." That may be, but chloroform killed a few people who got too strong a dose. I don't know what drug I was given. All I know is that a man in a white coat deftly inserted the

IV line into my arm while chatting about his dog. Then I conked out; then I woke up, minus one PT gland. A week earlier, a man in a suit at the front office asked me how I would pay for surgery. Then he asked me my religion. I should have said the Church of Anesthesiology. Anyone who's had surgery or serious dental work will understand this devotion.

The history of drugs that numb pain has not been a smooth road of soothed and delighted patients. Getting the right amount of a drug into a patient was not easy. I learned more about this problem at the Anaesthesia Heritage Centre in London. One display, the 1917 Boyle Machine, reminded me of a canning tool rather than a way to deliver nitrous oxide. Other devices looked like they came from the plumbing aisle of a hardware store. Or were props for a horror film. I'm quite sure one also played eight-track tapes. Another device had what looked like the valve on a bicycle tire and was the same green as a Bianchi bicycle.

One popular display showed the painkilling drugs used by famous people. Elvis liked Demerol, Judy Garland liked Seconal. Michael Jackson made propofol a household name. After the pop star's death, doctors could not convince some patients that the drug was safe. If I was to be given propofol, I didn't want to know.

In reading at the British Library about PT surgery, I learned that a local painkiller could be used, rather than one that knocks the patient out. With a local, the patient can breathe without a tube and talk to confirm that the vocal chords still work. A drawing in the book showed a man's head under a small tent during surgery with a local. A fan blew across his face to keep him from feeling trapped. "I suppose a local could be used," my surgeon said, "because you're thin. But I think you'd want to be out those few minutes." I assume the man was strapped down which would make this a poor choice for me. Better to be out like a light. Out like three good PT glands when the fourth one goes bad. Out while a man chats about his dog.

No Free Samples

Museums devoted to the science of anesthesia are more common than you might think, but London's museum might be the only one to include a 2.8-mile walking tour. I wanted to honor the history of this noble cause, so I started the self-guided tour with good cheer.

Stop number one was a limestone building with a nice bronze plaque devoted, I assumed, to mouthwash:

LORD LISTER

(1827 – 1912)

SURGEON

LIVED HERE

Lord Lister, I read in the tour brochure, was a fan of general anesthesia. He also cared about patient safety. Bravo! I said, moving on to number two. Here I admired a red stone building. The first major operation in England with general anesthesia took place here in 1846. A man's leg was removed. Then I read that *here* meant the area, not the red stone building. The original building was torn down. That's nice, I thought, and moved on.

Tour stop number three is the grand Bonham Carter House. Helena herself might have stepped out the front door into the set of a nineteenth-century English film. I read the fine print in my brochure. Again, in this general area— not this exact building—for the first time, a dental patient was given ether before having a tooth pulled. At the end of the block I came to stop number four, a brown brick building. James Robinson, who gave the ether to the dental patient at stop number three, lived here.

Reading ahead in the brochure, I knew that I could see the home of a surgeon who opposed the use of ether or chloroform for labor pain, never mind what Queen Victoria said. And I might see the site of the 1854 cholera outbreak, a side story in the history of anesthesia. And I could walk all the way to the home and workshop of a man who helped to introduce laughing gas as a painkiller. But alas, no free samples had been promised or delivered. And I was hungry after completing about one mile, so I quit the tour.

SIX

More Fun Than a Cast

"You were healthy until you met me," my husband says. He's right. When I left the hospital at birth, I never looked back. I rarely got colds. Nothing broke. Aspirin was a hard drug meant for severe pain. But of course, meeting him didn't make my PT gland go bad. We married at an age when we start that slow slide south. My rogue gland merely reminded me that a body is destined to fail. Not entirely a bad plan.

When I was young, I had a bit of envy for kids who showed up at school with a cast. Not that I wanted a broken arm or leg. But they had this aura about them. They'd been to some exotic place. For all I knew they'd joined some tribe that lived off the edge of my map. Or they'd been abducted by aliens, long before any of us knew that was an option. That plaster cast was proof.

I got over the envy when the kid with the cast started to scratch, digging into that dark cave between skin and plaster. But I saw that with illness or a break comes a new status. When my PT gland went bad, I knew I'd been struck. Not by lightning, but by something few friends knew anything about. More fun than a cast, my rogue gland. Not the level of adventure as the friend of a friend who lived through a grizzly bear attack and has claw scars to prove it. But something in between.

An Impressive Scar

Until recently, a PT surgeon cut across the patient's neck almost ear to ear. Then the surgeon pulled the skin apart, like opening a duffle bag, and looked for all four glands. That was the only way to find which one was enlarged with a tumor. Pictures of surgery done this way are spooky. The patient's face looks like it might peel off, as if the face is a mask. But this leaves an impressive scar.

Today a PT surgeon makes a one-inch or even smaller cut over the bad gland. When the neck is cut along a natural crease line, the scar is barely visible.

"I wouldn't have noticed your scar if you hadn't pointed it out," said one friend. "It looks like the kind of scratch you might get from a cat," said another.

A few days after the operation, my surgeon nodded and smiled at the good job he'd done. The scar looks like someone drew a picture of my neck, then drew over one small part of a crease line with the same pencil. He told me to put vitamin E on the scar to make it go away. But E is gooey stuff. I bought a bottle of capsules at the drug store and when I cut one open, a clear gold pus oozed out. I tried it once and didn't use it again. I don't care if I have a scar. If I didn't have one, what would I have to show for the whole event? How could I prove I'd been cut open—I know, a small cut, but still—and then walked away whole?

Hungry Bones

After my health-fair test showed I had high calcium, every medical person I saw asked me the same thing. Did I feel much fatigue? "Maybe," I always said. Doesn't everyone get tired? Sometimes late morning, late afternoon, always at night. Yeah, I got tired. I assumed getting older didn't help. Any kidney stones? was always the next question. Maybe I'd been lucky. Each time I heard this I vowed to drink more water and add cranberry juice to my diet.

Life post-surgery was better for me than it was for the patients at the Old Operating Theatre. The fatigue I didn't know I had was gone. Words or names that might have ambled into my brain as I spoke now raced to find their right place in a sentence. Too much calcium in the blood muddies the mind, but you wouldn't know it at the time. Like the bad joke about hitting your head against a wall—it feels good when it stops.

The first night after surgery I felt tingling in my face and arms. Then I remembered the paper I was given at the hospital warning me about this. I called my surgeon, as I'd been told. He said to take some calcium, suggesting Tums. The tingling went on for days. The PT glands that go dormant when one goes bad can take a while to start working again. This means blood calcium levels can drop. I worried they'd never work again and ate calcium like it was candy.

The worst thing to do if you don't feel well is to trawl online for answers. I found people who had PT surgery and never felt right. When friends asked how surgery went, I saw how I could turn illness into my whole identity. A few days after surgery, my husband asked if I'd like to go with him on a work trip to New York. I asked if I could decide after I saw my surgeon and the results of my next blood test. "I might not do anything normal ever again," I said, "because I'll be lugging around calcium, like those people dragging around their oxygen tanks."

My surgeon said I had Hungry Bones Syndrome. This sounded like I had a blues band living in my body. "B . . . B . . . B . . . B . . . Bad to the bone" kept going through my head. I thought of my bones as calcium-deprived thugs, grabbing ice cream cones out of the mouths of babes. My blood test showed that all my numbers were hyper-normal. Calcium level smack dab in the middle. Same with the PT hormone. I was still worried about all the tingling. My doctor saw my normal calcium results and turned his worries to my high cholesterol on the same report. I've seen worse, I wanted to say, like I'm some veteran, and he's the new guy who's never seen heavy action.

SEVEN

Slimy Things in Jars

During World War II, fifteen thousand people died when German bombs hit London. On one of the worst nights, May 11, 1941, a bomb hit the Hunterian Museum in the Royal College of Surgeons. Friends of the museum sifted through the rubble. Two-thirds of the collection was destroyed. But someone found a large jar, the surface white with ash. The neck of Richard Owen's rhino with the pea-sized PT gland was saved.

I went to the Hunterian to see the gland. This is the best museum in London, and it's free. Plus there are no long lines of tourists waiting to get in. Compare that to Madame Tussauds wax museum or the Tower of London. As you enter the doors of the Royal College, you can think of all the people waiting in long lines. Here you're greeted by someone who seems pleased to see you. You're given the chance to go to a cloak room to deposit your cloak. Then you're directed upstairs to the museum.

The best display—except for the rhino neck—is inside the main door to the left. I call it the "Filleted Man." It's just like it sounds—a man who's been filleted and gutted like a fish. All the bones are gone, the inner organs too, and the skin and muscles. What's left are the arteries and veins spread out on a slab of wood in the shape of a man. I couldn't take my eyes off the lacy body. A spider might have spun him. But I had a mission. Find that rhino neck.

The museum hosts exhibits of current interest, such as "Anatomy of an Athlete" during London's Summer Olympics. But what the first-time visitor remembers are the jars of body parts. The human fetuses. The giant toad cut open, like zipping off a jacket, to reveal his insides. The skull of a boy with two brains. Thousands of jars. My vision narrowed. I missed the math expert's brain, the gray wolf embryo. My mind shoved these into a *not rhino* corner. And all the shelves in the museum were filled with *not rhino* jars. The museum is a trove of wet slimy things in jars, but not the slimy thing I was looking for.

A Gusto for Body Parts

A man at the front desk told me whom to contact to see jars of organs kept in storage. Back at the hotel, I e-mailed the museum, carefully asking to see the rhino neck. Maybe my reason for wanting to see Richard Owen's rhino would not sound important enough. Maybe they're mobbed with requests like mine. I could be turned down. Instead, Martyn Cooke, Head of Conservation, suggested a time and day and came to the front desk when I arrived.

Martyn led me down a back hallway, then through a door into a storage room. He walked down one aisle and found the right shelf. After pulling out the jar with the rhino neck, he set it on a table for me to see. It looks like a lava lamp. The jar is about the size of the body of a table lamp. The rhino neck is a greenish off-white. Though solid, it looks like it could break apart in the next moment into ever-changing liquid blobs. The PT gland, round like a pea, might already have started to break away. I stared, imprinting the details of the waxy shape on my mind. Like staring at a sunset to fill up with beauty, I filled up with the whole odd history of this neck and gland.

Though I could have stared at the neck for a very long time, I didn't want to impose any longer on Martyn. On the same shelf as the rhino neck, he'd seen another jar with a leak—an ovary from an ostrich also dissected by Richard Owen. Martyn thanked me for prompting this discovery. After putting the rhino neck back where it belonged, he took me to his workroom to show me the process of taking care of the specimens. I learned that the care of them is a dying art. Pitch, pig bladder, and linen thread soaked in beeswax are part of the old process. When jars are resealed now, the new seal is shaped by hand and then painted black to match the original. The care Martyn and his staff take includes making new labels look like the old ones. But now, instead of hand-printed italic lettering, he prints from a computer font.

When I left, I glanced at my watch and saw that I'd stayed for over two hours. I wonder if Martyn wished I'd left earlier. But I'm grateful he didn't hurry me out the door. He let me dip into Richard

Owen's life and steep in his gusto for body parts. Richard Owen left no evidence that he cared much about that tiny rhino gland, the last body part. But one day I imagined Richard being given my excised gland, my "Gland of Caroline." I saw him drop it in a liquid-filled jar and seal the lid. Then he fondly wrote on a label with a pen dipped in ink. He gave the organ a number, one higher than the last specimen of his career.

THANK YOU
Brian Bouldrey
Mary Brown
Martyn Cooke
Trish O'Hare
Seth Peterson
Nicholas Woolf

AND

The Anaesthesia Heritage Centre
The British Library
The Hunterian Museum
The Old Operating Theatre
The Wellcome Library

REFERENCES

Ochsner, Albert J., and Ralph L. Thompson. *The Surgery and Pathology of the Thyroid and Parathyroid Glands*. London: George Keener, 1910.

Oertli, Daniel, and Robert Udelsman, eds. *Surgery of the Thyroid and Parathyroid Glands*. Berlin: Springer-Verlag, 2007.

Owen, Richard S. *The Life of Richard Owen*. London: John Murray, 1894.

Owen, Richard. "On the Anatomy of the Indian Rhinoceros (Rh. Unicornis, L.)." *Transactions of the Zoological Society of London* IV (1851): 31–58.